For Robert, Brian, and Lavinia.
—L. S.

To the polar bear and the indigenous people of the Arctic.
—L. D.

SPECIAL THANKS TO THE STAFF AT THE CHURCHILL NORTHERN STUDIES CENTRE FOR REVIEWING THE MANUSCRIPT,
AND ESPECIALLY TO DR. NICK LUNN OF THE CANADIAN WILDLIFE SERVICE FOR SHARING HIS EXPERTISE,
AND TO MELISSA GIBBONS FOR HER ASSISTANCE.

Library of Congress Cataloging-in-Publication Data:
Stafford, Liliana
The Snow Bear / written by Liliana Stafford; illustrated by Lambert Davis.—1st American ed.
p.   cm.
Summary: A lifelong friendship develops between a polar bear and Bruun, an Inuit boy. After Bruun saves her from
starvation and she, in turn, saves him from a blizzard, eventually they are separated and don't meet again until Bruun is a
man.
ISBN 0-439-26977-6
1. Polar bear—Juvenile fiction. [1. Polar bear—Fiction. 2. Inuit—Fiction. 3. Friendship—Fiction. 4. Eskimos—Fiction.
5. Bears—Fiction. 6. Canada—Fiction.] I. Davis, Lambert, ill. II. Title.   PZ10.3.S7794 Sn 2000
[E]—dc21   00-063503

10 9 8 7 6 5 4 3 2 1   01 02 03 04 05
Printed in Hong Kong
First American edition, October 2001
The text type was set in 17-point Truesdell.

The Snow Bear

By **LILIANA STAFFORD**

Illustrated by **LAMBERT DAVIS**

SCHOLASTIC PRESS · NEW YORK

The bear came into town in the autumn to feed at the dump.
Her cubs had been killed by hunters and she was weary.
Only Bruun saw her plight. She is too thin, he thought.

"If she comes again they will lock her up," his father said.
"The town is no place for bears."

"Will they feed her then?" Bruun asked.

"No," said his father. "It is natural for bears to fast through the
warmer months. They will keep her in the bear jail till the sea-ice
freezes over and then she will be set free. She'll go quicker if she
is hungry. Feeding her would only make her want to stay."

The bear did come again and they locked her in the bear jail.
   Bruun understood the wisdom of his father's words but his
heart went out to the bear. Her hunger is too much, he thought,
and he stole a fish.

"Eat," whispered Bruun. "It is for you. I will bring you more."

The snow bear was grateful. The food gave her back her strength and the boy filled the space in her heart where her cubs had been. From then on she waited for his visits.

When winter came and the sea-ice was frozen over, the snow bear
was released from the jail.

"Go quickly," Bruun said. But the snow bear wouldn't go.

"She must leave," said his mother, "or die. The town is no place
for bears."

Bruun put on his bear-skin coat and boots. "I will take her."

The boy and the bear left the town. Their footprints were twin
tracks in the snow.

Out on the ice they were alone.

"Go," Bruun said. "This is your place. If I stay I will freeze."

But the bear refused to go.

Then a blizzard came in from the north and covered their tracks. It blew so strong and so wild that Bruun became lost and feared for his life.

To keep Bruun safe the snow bear lay down, offering her warmth, and the boy lay next to her. The snow began to cover them and Bruun felt sleepy. It was quiet and peaceful under the snow.

When the blizzard was over the snow bear brought a seal cub
to Bruun. He was too hungry to say no.

In the weeks that followed, Bruun stayed with the bear, rarely
leaving the den.

When spring came he followed her onto the ice, watching while she waited for seals and resting with her after the kill. He learned how to jump the ice floes and how to sniff the wind for possible prey. And when the bear washed, he washed, rubbing his face and hands in the snow.

Other bears came to the ice to hunt. Many were adult males
eager to mate. The snow bear felt their presence. She knew it
was time to push away her cub.

But Bruun wouldn't go. He lay down in the snow.

The snow bear led him back to the town, as if to say, This is your place. But Bruun refused to go.

The hunters were out with their dogs and harpoons. They saw Bruun and the bear.

"No, don't!" Bruun yelled.

The snow bear escaped and the hunters took Bruun back to
the town.

There was great rejoicing that the boy was alive, but Bruun
did not join in. He dreamed only of being back with the snow
bear and refused to take off his bear-skin coat.

All summer he pined for the bear, and in the autumn he
watched for her at the dump. When winter came, he made
the long journey out onto the ice to find her.

It was spring when he finally saw her. She was with her cubs.

"Take me back," he whispered, but the bear walked on, leading her new family out onto the ice to hunt.

When Bruun tried to follow she chased him away.

Bruun quietly turned back to the town.

Many years went by and Bruun grew to be a man. He became
the best hunter the town had ever known, always hunting in
the old ways, never with a gun.

And one day he saw the snow bear—still hunting for seals.

"Hello, old friend," he murmured. "You taught me well."

The snow bear walked toward him and Bruun saw that she was old and starving. He knew she would not survive the summer.

He raised his harpoon.

Then he lowered it again.

"Come," he said to the aging bear. "I have skills enough for both of us."

Bruun and the snow bear spent the summer and autumn together. And when winter came they made the long journey out onto the ice.

The snow bear urged Bruun to go, for she only wished to sleep.

"No, I won't go," said Bruun. And he stayed with the bear till
she was as cold and silent as the snow. Then Bruun made the
long journey back to the town alone.

The snow bear had been his friend and now she was gone. But her memory lived in the stories Bruun told his own son, when they went out onto the ice together.

When I wrote *The Snow Bear* I had been thinking about humankind's interaction with the natural world, particularly with animals. I had written a number of notes under the heading "Shelter" but nothing concrete had formed. Then one night a picture came into my head of a polar bear who was in some kind of trouble. She had been caught in a storm and her cubs were dead. At the same moment, the words "The Snow Bear" were there and I knew it was the beginning of a story.

I imagined a relationship between a boy and a polar bear, but I wasn't sure how it might begin. Then while doing research, I read about the "bear jail" and knew I had found their connection.

In reality, a boy and a polar bear could not have an intimate relationship like the one in the story. With their thick white fur and black noses, polar bears appear cute and cuddly but are really wild animals, not domesticated pets. If provoked they can be extremely dangerous. The polar bear is the largest carnivore on land. A female polar bear, like the snow bear, standing on her hind legs could tower up to eight feet tall and weigh as much as 650 pounds. A male polar bear can weigh more than twice that!

Gathering consistent information about polar bears can be difficult. Although polar bear scientists have learned quite a bit about polar bear populations over the past twenty years, the numbers still vary. There are several reasons for this: The vastness of the polar bear's habitats, nature's camouflage (white fur on white ice), their strength as swimmers, and their ability to cover large distances quickly, all contribute to the complexity in locating them and tracking their behaviors. In addition, polar bears can survive conditions that humans cannot withstand. To complicate the situation even more, male polar bears' necks are wider than their heads, so if a tracking collar is put on them, it just falls off. Therefore, depending on the source, there are approximately 22,000 to 27,000 polar bears in the world.

I modeled the town where Bruun lives on a northern Canadian town: Churchill, Manitoba. The locals of Churchill proudly call their community *The Polar Bear Capital of the World* and it is a favorite destination for tourists. They ride in the specially-designed tundra vehicles that allow them to safely watch the polar bears in their native habitat.

As in the story, polar bears spend the winter months on the sea-ice hunting seals, their major source of nutrition. (Unlike other bears, polar bears don't hibernate in the winter, with the exception of some pregnant females.) They also go swimming and can travel up to sixty miles at a time. In the warmer months, when the ice (which is bigger than the state of Texas) begins to thaw, the polar bears of Churchill are forced onto shore where they begin their fast, until the ice freezes again. However, not all polar bear populations spend the summer on land. In some regions they simply retreat with the ice as it recedes.

Because the sea-ice has begun to melt earlier each year, which is often attributed to global warming, polar bears are deprived of valuable feeding time in the spring. As a result, sometimes they do not have enough stored fat to nourish themselves through their fast. When this occurs, some bears will eat berries and grasses, though all bears prefer meat. Their keen sense of smell, reaching as far away as ten miles, helps them detect food. Often this brings them into town and straight to the town dump (just as the snow bear did) or to a family's garbage can. Over time, the Churchill dump has been polar bear-proofed and is monitored to keep the polar bears from scavenging, but they still come to town. Can you imagine turning a street corner to find a polar bear in your front yard? The townspeople of Churchill can.

Though my story is fiction, "bear jails" are real. The bear jail in Churchill was established in 1982 in an effort to protect the townspeople from the polar bears and the polar bears from human harm. At one time, as in my story, polar bears were held indefinitely at the bear jail until winter came and the ice was frozen again. Today, however, the polar bears are only detained for about a month before being released into the wild. Their incarceration is meant to deter them from returning to town. While at the bear jail, the polar bears are given water, but not food. As Bruun's father points out in the story, "Feeding her would only make her want to stay." It is more important to help the polar bears thrive within their own habitat, rather than letting them get comfortable in ours.

In an effort to keep the polar bear from becoming extinct, all the countries that are home to polar bears (Canada, Russia, Denmark, Norway, and the United States) signed the Agreement on the Conservation of Polar Bears and their Habitats in 1973. This banned the hunting of polar bears, except by local people using traditional methods in the exercise of their traditional rights.

The Snow Bear came in response to my searching for answers about nature, tradition, and the power of love. I hope her story will stir others to do the same.